Great Big Animals

GIGANTIC WHALE SHARKS

By Stephanie Carrington

Please visit our website, www.garethstevens.com. For a free color catalog of all our high-quality books, call toll free 1-800-542-2595 or fax 1-877-542-2596.

Cataloging-in-Publication Data

Names: Carrington, Stephanie.
Title: Gigantic whale sharks / Stephanie Carrington.
Description: New York : Gareth Stevens Publishing, 2018. | Series: Great big animals | Includes index.
Identifiers: ISBN 9781538208991 (pbk.) | ISBN 9781538209011 (library bound) | ISBN 9781538209004 (6 pack)
Subjects: LCSH: Whale shark–Juvenile literature.
Classification: LCC QL638.95.R4 C37 2018 | DDC 597.3–dc23

First Edition

Published in 2018 by
Gareth Stevens Publishing
111 East 14th Street, Suite 349
New York, NY 10003

Editor: Kate Mikoley
Designer: Sarah Liddell

Photo credits: Cover, p. 1 Krzysztof Odziomek/Shutterstock.com; p. 5 Liquid Productions, LLC/Shutterstock.com; p. 7 Rich Carey/Shutterstock.com; p. 9 David Evison/Shutterstock.com; pp. 11, 24 (tail) Chatuphon Neelasri/Shutterstock.com; p. 13 OceanImpressions/Shutterstock.com; pp. 15, 17 Andrea Izzotti/Shutterstock.com; p. 19 Brandelet/Shutterstock.com; p. 21 Fata Morgana by Andrew Marriott/Shutterstock.com; pp. 23, 24 (plankton) Dmitri Ma/Shutterstock.com.

Printed in the United States of America

CPSIA compliance information: Batch #CW18GS: For further information contact Gareth Stevens, New York, New York at 1-800-542-2595.

Contents

Giant Fish 4
Gray and White. 16
What's for Dinner?. 20
Words to Know 24
Index. 24

Whale sharks are
not whales.
They are big sharks!

They are
the biggest fish.

They are as big
as a bus!

They have big tails.

They live
in warm water.

They are very heavy. Some weigh more than 20 tons.

They are often gray.

Some have white bits called spots.

They eat a lot of food!

They eat small animals.
These are
called plankton.

Words to Know

plankton

tail

Index

fish 6

plankton 22

spots 18

tail 10